This book belongs to

...........Mhairi...............

To Sinéad Murphy

A DORLING KINDERSLEY BOOK

First published in Great Britain in 1998 by Dorling Kindersley Limited,
9 Henrietta Street, London WC2E 8PS
Visit us on the World Wide Web at http://www.dk.com

A CIP catalogue record for this book is available from the British Library.

ISBN 0 - 7513 - 7064 - 9 (hardback)
ISBN 0 - 7513 - 7185 - 8 (paperback)

Colour Reproduction by DOT Gradations

Printed in Hong Kong by Wing King Tong

2 4 6 8 10 9 7 5 3

Caterpillar's wish

Mary Murphy

Caterpillar and Bee and Ladybird live in a lovely garden.

When Bee and Ladybird
fly away, Caterpillar
stays behind.

"I wish I could fly too," she says.

But Bee and Ladybird
always come back.

One day, when
Bee and Ladybird
come home,
Caterpillar
is gone.

"Do you know where she is, Snail?" asks Bee.

"Caterpillar is in this cocoon," says Snail. "She is sleeping and dreaming."

Bee and Ladybird visit the cocoon every day. Until...

Who is that peeping out?
"It is me at last," says Caterpillar.

"But now my name is Butterfly...

and I can fly!"

Other Toddler books to collect:

BABY LOVES by Michael Lawrence,
illustrated by Adrian Reynolds

THE PIG WHO WISHED by Joyce Dunbar,
illustrated by Selina Young

PANDA BIG AND PANDA SMALL
by Jane Cabrera

I'M TOO BUSY by Helen Stephens